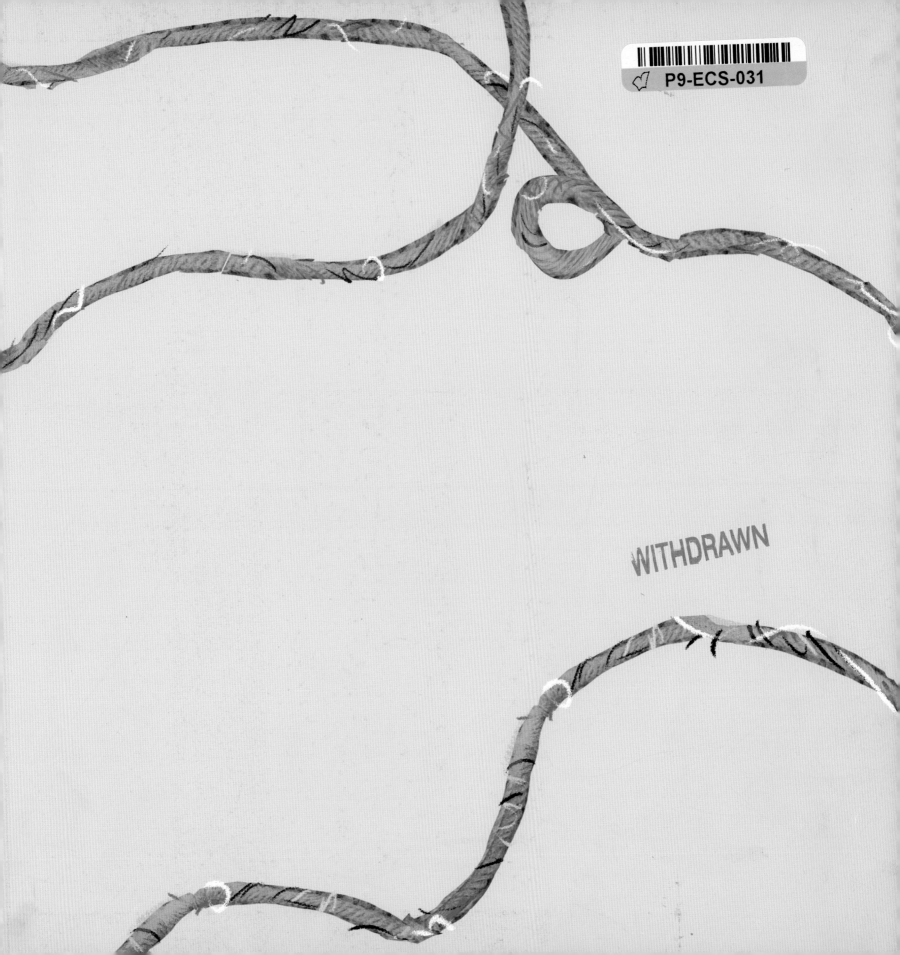

P9-ECS-031

WITHDRAWN

About This Book

The illustrations for this book were done digitally and with photo collaging.
The text was set in the author's hand lettering.

Copyright © 2021 by Loryn Brantz

Cover illustration copyright © 2021 by Loryn Brantz. Cover design by
Marci Sanders and David Hastings. • Cover copyright © 2021 by Hachette Book Group, Inc.

Hachette Book Group supports the right to free expression and the value of copyright. The purpose of copyright
is to encourage writers and artists to produce the creative works that enrich our culture.

The scanning, uploading, and distribution of this book without permission is a theft of the author's
intellectual property. If you would like permission to use material from the book (other than for review purposes),
please contact permissions@hbgusa.com. Thank you for your support of the author's rights.

Little, Brown and Company • Hachette Book Group • 1290 Avenue of the Americas, New York, NY 10104
Visit us at LBYR.com

First Edition: January 2021

Little, Brown and Company is a division of Hachette Book Group, Inc.
The Little, Brown name and logo are trademarks of Hachette Book Group, Inc.

The publisher is not responsible for websites (or their content) that are not owned by the publisher.

Blanket texture copyright © Floor Vanden Berghe/Creative Market • Texture on tree copyright © Salah/Motosha • Texture on
cocoon copyright © Dmytro Synelnychenko/123rf • Wood texture around chalkboard © Freecreatives • Texture on chalkboard
© Wallpaperset • Texture on lab coat © Mifti-Stock/DeviantArt • Various other textures © Lee Tomilson, www.gullrat.com, and
Company Folders, Inc.

Library of Congress Cataloging-in-Publication Data • Names: Brantz, Loryn, author. • Title: Blanket : journey to extreme coziness
/ by Loryn Brantz. • Description: [New York : Little, Brown and Company, 2021] • Audience: Ages 3-5. • Summary: A young child
shows how to make a safe, secure cocoon from a favorite fuzzy blanket, then imagines adventures before and after emerging
from it. • Identifiers: LCCN 2019054750 • ISBN 978-0-7595-5479-5 (hardback) • Subjects: CYAC: Blankets—Fiction. • Imagination—
Fiction. • Security (Psychology)—Fiction • Classification: LCC PZ7.B737586 BI 2021 • DDC [E]—dc23
LC record available at https://lccn.loc.gov/2019054750

ISBN 978-0-7595-5479-5

PRINTED IN MALAYSIA

TWP

10 9 8 7 6 5 4 3 2 1

BLANKET

Journey to Extreme Coziness

Loryn Brantz

L B

Little, Brown and Company

New York   Boston

For Deb, the coziness Queen

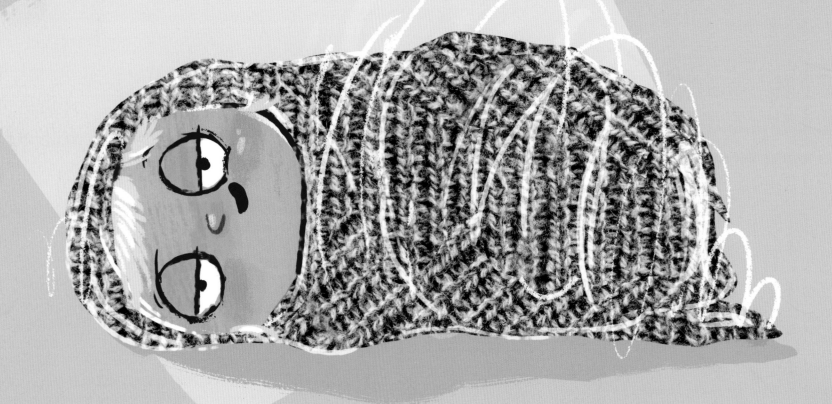

Shhh! Be very quiet.

Watch as the caterpillar hangs from that branch. It's making a warm and cozy cocoon.

To make your very own snuggly, cuddly blanket cocoon, follow these easy steps.

STEP 1: Find your most favorite blanket.

STEP 2: Lay it out on the floor.

STEP 3: Lie down on the very edge of it.

STEP 4: NOW ROLL!!!

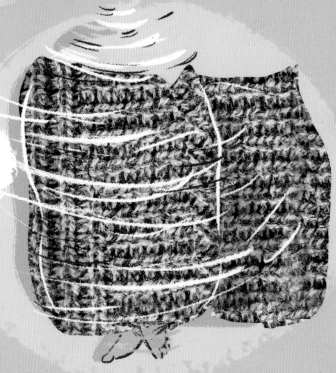

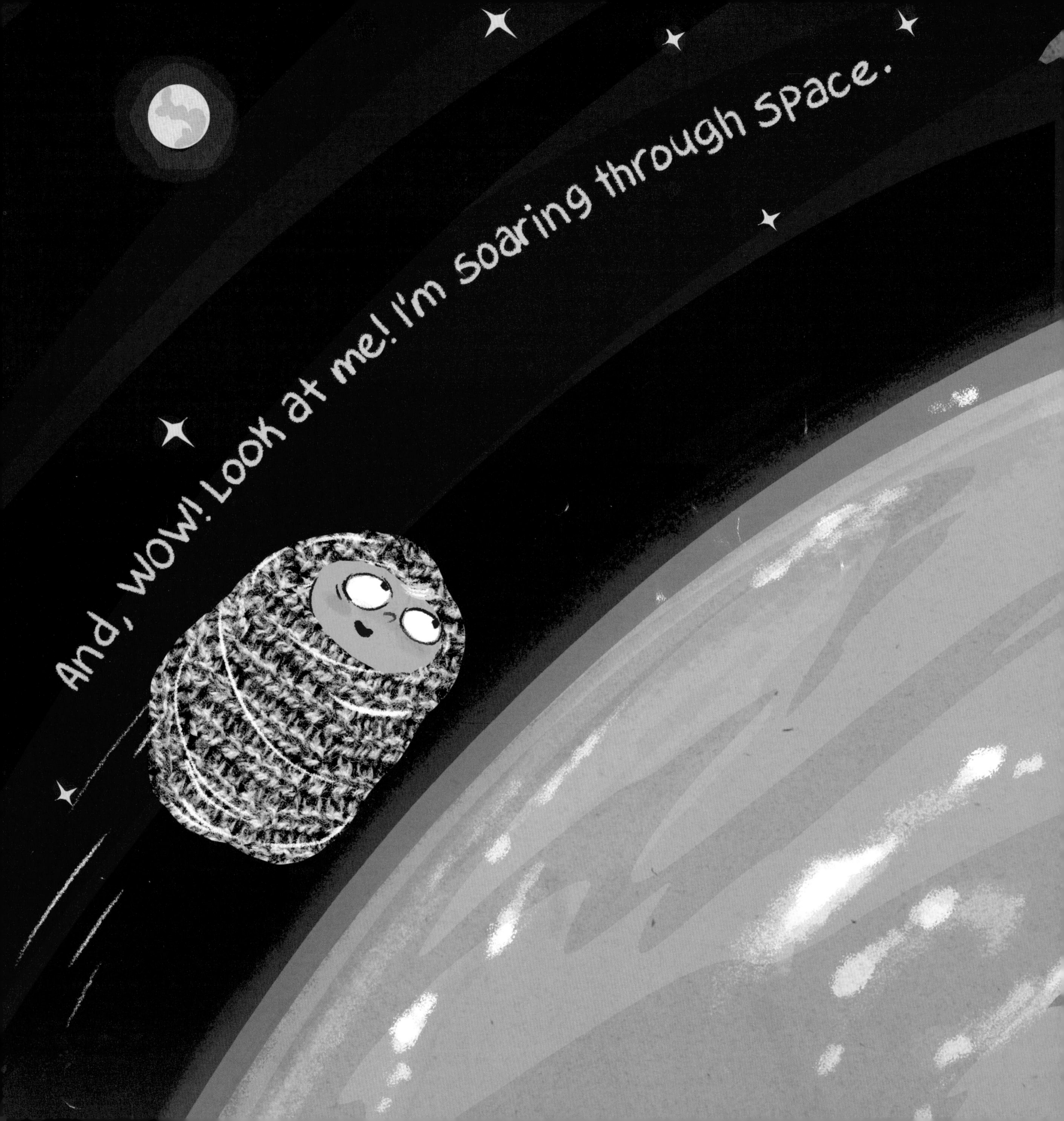

And, WOW! Look at me! I'm soaring through space.

And running through the rain forest...

Now I'm inside an igloo covered in snow . . .

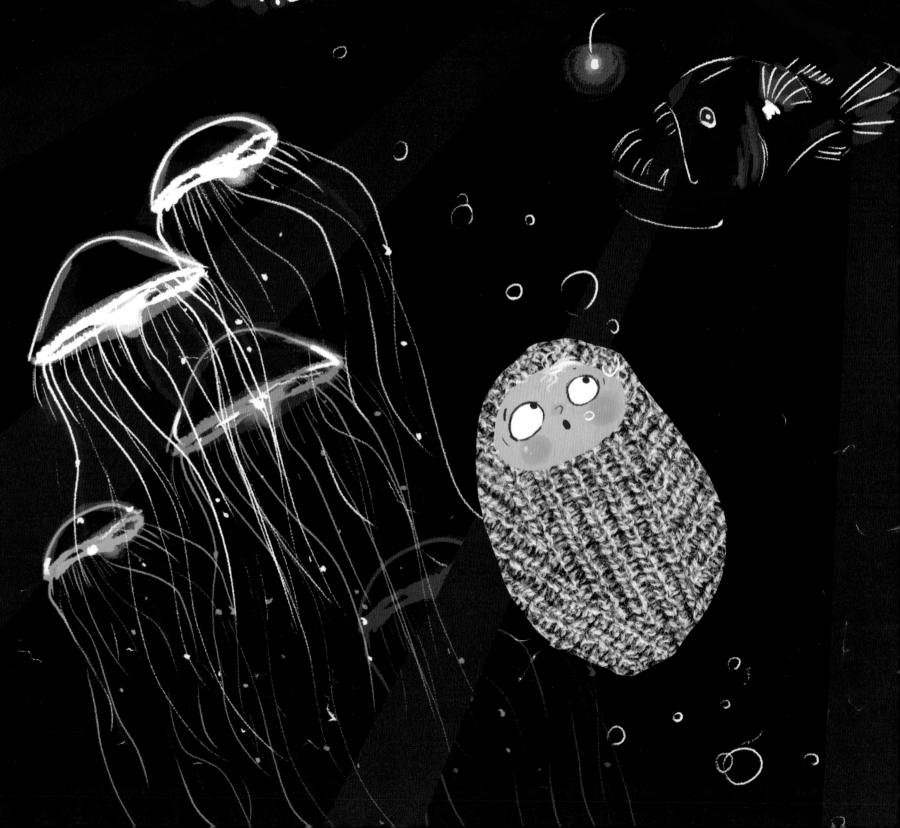

and under the deep blue sea.

What is going
to happen
when we leave our
blanket cocoons?

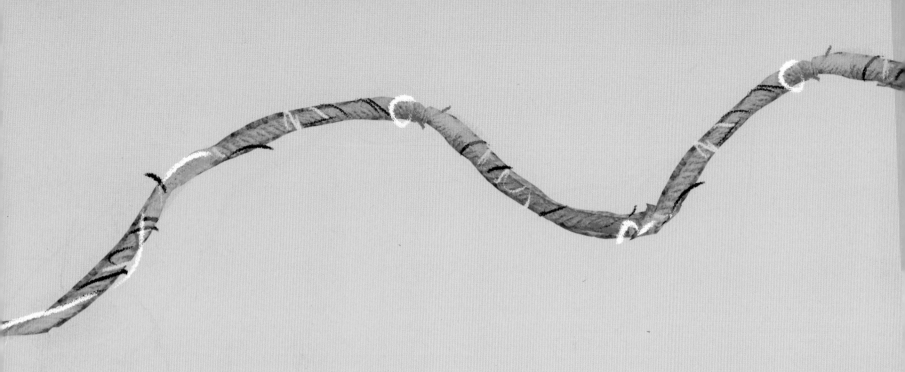

Not Knowing what will

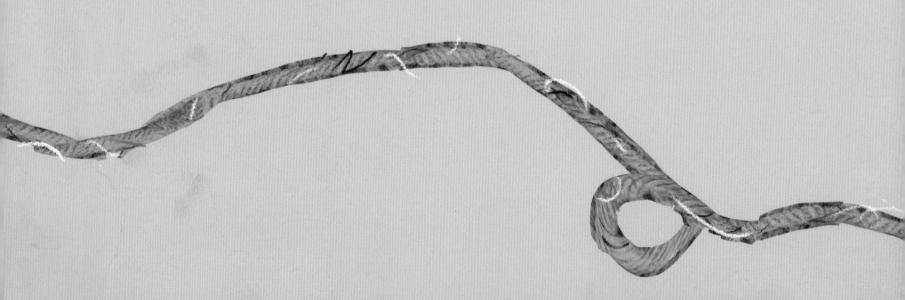

happen is kind of scary.

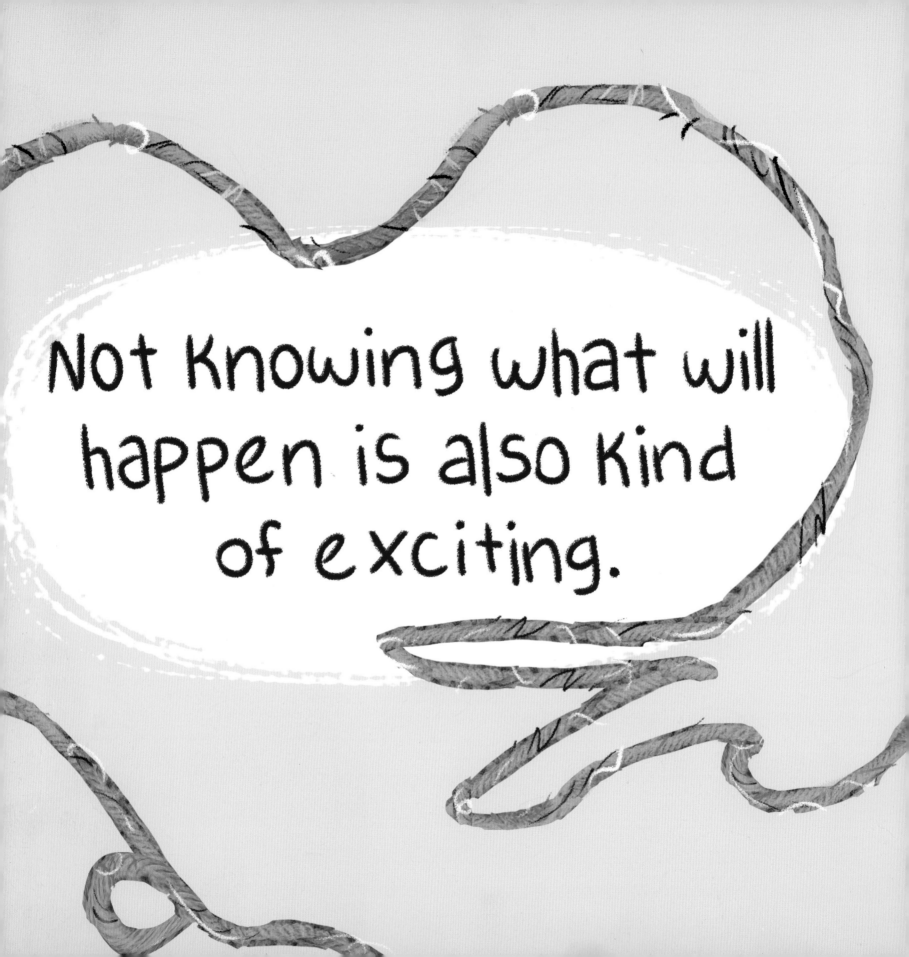

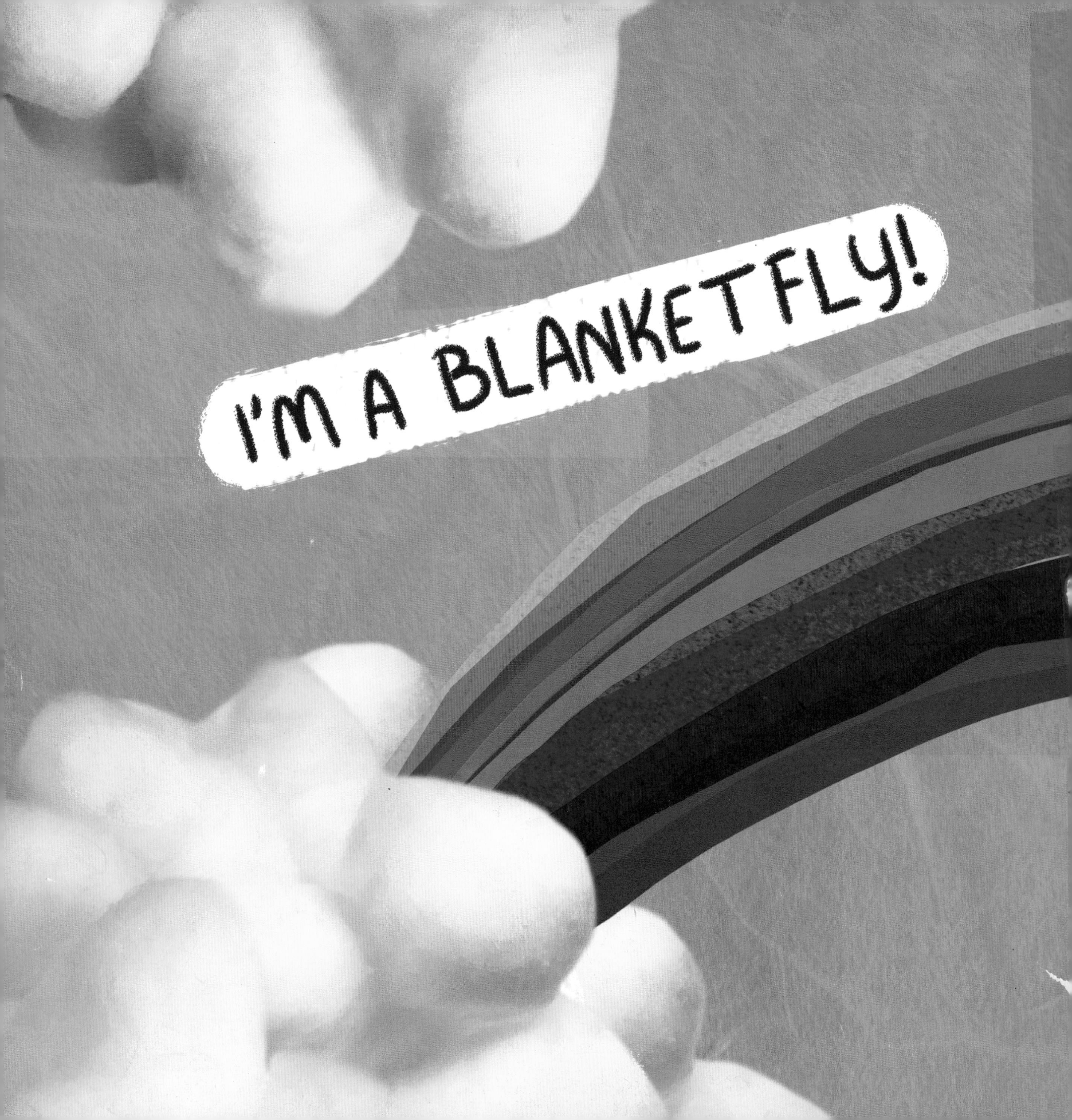
I'M A BLANKETFLY!

What did you become? A blanketfly too?

Or a blanket cat?

Or a blanket bunny?

Or the best thing of all ... the amazing you?!

31901066374531